by Jan Carr
Pictures by Frank Hill

ISBN 0-590-33703-3

12 1 10 9 8 7 6 5 4 3 2 1   4   6 7 9/8 0 1/9
Printed in the U.S.A.   24

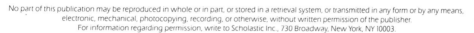

SCHOLASTIC INC.
New York Toronto London Auckland Sydney

It was cold and dark that morning in Rivertown — cold, and dark, and early. In her bedroom at the Lost Lambs Home for Orphans, Nurse Plumtree heard a strange, loud sound. YEOWL. It was coming from outside. YEOOWL . . . YEOOOWL.

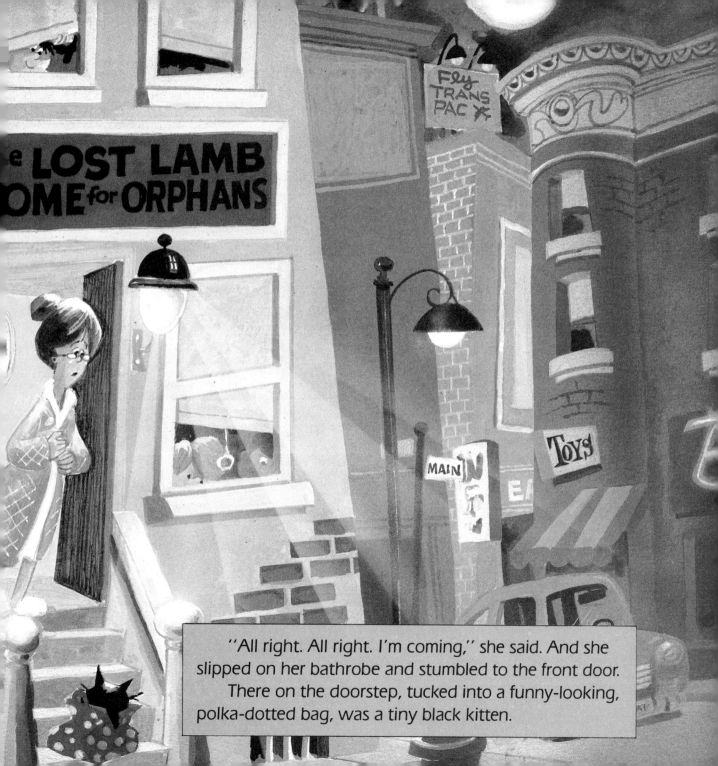

"All right. All right. I'm coming," she said. And she slipped on her bathrobe and stumbled to the front door. There on the doorstep, tucked into a funny-looking, polka-dotted bag, was a tiny black kitten.

"Why, what have we here?" said Nurse Plumtree. Pinned to the kitten's bag was a note.

"Well, I'll be . . ." said Nurse Plumtree. "Poor little fellow."
And she brought Felix in out of the cold.

Nurse Plumtree carried Felix into the kitchen and gave him a dish of warm milk.

Then she bundled him up in a soft, fleecy blanket, and put him in the nursery.

Felix felt warm and cozy. And not the least bit sleepy.
He sang a little song to himself as the first rays of morning
light began to shine through the nursery window.

The Lost Lambs Home for Orphans was just the perfect place for Felix. The little children were always peeking into his bag to see how he was . . .

or where he was.

Felix was very playful, and he soon developed into a good jumper. . .
and a very good climber.

His favorite game was "Hide and Seek."

Felix always hid in the most unusual places.

Sometimes Nurse Plumtree would get mad at Felix. There
was the time, for instance, when he ate all the tunafish.
And the time he drank everyone's lunch milk.

And then, of course, there was that time when he and the others went digging for a buried treasure . . . in Nurse Plumtree's garden!

But Nurse Plumtree never stayed mad at Felix for very long. Something about the way he'd smile up at her, even when she was yelling at him, something about the impish twinkle in his eyes. . . .

"Felix," Nurse Plumtree would say. "If you weren't so cute, you'd be in a <u>lot</u> of trouble."

Nurse Plumtree wasn't the only one who loved Felix. All the other little orphans loved him, too. "Sit by me at lunch, Felix?" one would ask. Or, "Felix, could you help me tie my shoe?" And Felix always would.

He taught the new, little ones how to play marbles and checkers and "Go Fish."

And he told the sad ones funny stories that made them laugh. Just about everyone at the Lost Lambs Home for Orphans thought that Felix was the most wonderful cat in the whole world.

Though life at the Home was kind to Felix, as he got a little older, he was not altogether happy. What he really wanted, what he wanted more than anything, was to be adopted.

Other orphans got adopted. Felix watched it happen.

A couple would come, and they would meet all the kids, and right away they would like one better than all the rest.

"Oh, George, look at the one with the curly red hair," the woman might say. "Isn't he just adorable?"

And then they'd take him home with them.

Felix tried all kinds of things in hopes that someone would adopt him. He sang songs when the people came. He did tricks. But still, Felix was never chosen.

On his sixth birthday, Felix was still living at the Orphan
Home. Nurse Plumtree and his friends, those friends who were
still left, made a big birthday party for him.

But Felix did not feel like having a happy birthday.

"I don't belong here," Felix thought. "I never did. It's all some horrible mistake. My real parents are probably worried sick about me. They're probably famous . . . or even royalty!

"I bet my father's really a king, and my mother's really a queen. I am probably a prince, stolen at birth, and forced to live all my royal days alone, in an orphan home!"

But Felix's wild dreams didn't make him feel much better. He longed for a real mother, a furry one, that he didn't have to share with everybody else. He also wanted a dad — the swell kind, like the ones he saw on TV — who'd pat him on the back and say,

That night, after Felix's party, Nurse Plumtree was kept awake for many hours by Felix's sad, lonely yowling.

But then, the next morning, some new people arrived, looking to adopt a child. And this time, when the woman said, "Oh, Harvey, look at <u>that</u> little one. Isn't he adorable?" she was pointing right at Felix!

Suddenly Felix felt scared.

"Oh, you'll <u>love</u> this one," said Nurse Plumtree, pushing Felix forward. "He's a <u>very</u> good eater . . . and a very good, er . . . climber . . . and a — why, he's just our favorite little Felix!"

"Felix," said the woman lovingly, "what a beautiful name. He's the one we want."

Nurse Plumtree packed Felix's clothes in his bag, gave him a big kiss, and sent him on his way.

And so Felix finally got a home,   and a real mom and dad.

Felix loved his new life. He never let his mom and dad out of his sight.

"Hey, Mom. Mom! Watch this!" Felix would say. Or, "Dad. DAD! Look at me!"

Felix even liked saying their names, over and over again. Mom and Dad, Mom and Dad.

And they, in turn, liked saying his.
"Finish your milk, Felix."
"Don't forget to wash behind your ears, Felix."
"Don't claw the curtains . . ."

Sometimes when Felix had to pick up his toys — all by himself,
or practice his clarinet <u>before</u> he was allowed to watch TV...
Felix would get mad at his mom and dad.

And sometimes Felix's mother and father would even get mad at Felix — and send him to his room.

It was then that Felix would remember the wonderful life he had had at the Lost Lambs Home for Orphans.

"Nurse Plumtree was never mad at me," Felix would think. "And she <u>never</u> sent me to my room!"

But no one in Felix's family ever stayed mad for very long. After a while, Felix's mom might knock on his door and say, "I've got something for you!"

And it would be a tunafish sandwich, with lots of mayonnaise and no celery — just the way Felix liked it.

Then Felix's dad might poke his head in and say, "I was thinking you might be ready for a story about now." And Felix would climb right up on his lap.

After he was tucked in and all the lights were out (except for the one in the hall), Felix would lie in bed thinking about his parents' good-night hugs.

"I'm so cozy," he'd say.

And then, Felix the Cat would purr just like a little kitten and sing himself to sleep . . .

with the happiest little song.

to be continued . . .